WALKING OUR TALK

THE ULTIMATE GUIDE TO
SELF-DISCOVERY

FATMATA TARAWALLEY

ISBN: 0979520010
ISBN-13: 9780979520013

For information and permission to reproduce selections from this book, contact ftarawal@hotmail.com. Printed in the United States of America.

DEDICATION

This book is dedicated to my mother, Mary, who has endured the many curve balls that life has thrown her way. During the rough years, she kept her head high and rose above the tide, because for her, every day brought a new beginning.

Thanks for not giving up on yourself or your children.

CONTENTS

INTRODUCTION
SELF-DISCOVERY

Breaking news: According to the International Broadcasting Corporation (IBC), two European Scientists have identified the magic formula for happiness.

According to scientists, a person can achieve such happiness simply by taking one pill a day for a week. The medicine retools the brain into thinking positively, and to look for the unseen benefit within each situation, which in turn leaves no room for negativity and unhappiness.

Imagine such a discovery for a moment. Now visualize the pandemonium spreading across the globe as masses of people fight over this precious commodity. Some people will pay any amount to obtain this formula. People will line-up for miles just to get their hands on this magic formula but they suddenly realize it was just a dream.

The fact is happiness cannot be achieved through a one-size-fits-all formula. To gain happiness and inner peace, we must first seek awareness of who we are and what our purpose in life may be. To gain this perspective, we must each go through a process of self-discovery.

Self-discovery allows us to find the core of our being. When we are comfortable with the person staring back at us in the mirror, then and only then, can we deal with the mixed messages we as individuals receive from society. We can then select the messages that promote and advance our individual lives and discard the messages that set us back. Once we are comfortable with ourselves, we can make such decisions with ease.

In our quest to find happiness, peace and love, we sometimes sought answers in self-help books. Regrettably, these books are quick to point out our faults, but leave us without adequate solutions to our problems. In this book, *Walking Our Talk: the Ultimate Guide to Self-Discovery,* we will learn how to self-diagnose our own faults and create meaningful solutions based on our personal experiences and the experiences of those around us. We will each learn to change our future path by creating a viable business plan for life. We may even seek professional help if necessary.

In my homeland, Liberia, most people cannot afford to seek professional help so they learn to solve their problems using one of two techniques. They either figure it out on their own or seek the wisdom and knowledge of their wise elders.

For example, Africans put a considerable amount of emphasis on the "seniority rule." This rule is there to prevent young people from challenging their elders and those in authority. Most Africans believes this social order promotes respect within the society. This does not mean that young people cannot express their feelings because they can, but only in a respectful manner.

To Western thinkers, this rule might sound odd or old-fashioned, but I can assure the skeptics among me that it does bear merit. All it takes is an open mind to grasp the possibilities and wonders life has to offer. We suggest trying this within your family for a month or two. Let everyone know about the 'seniority rule' experiment and ask him or her to participate fully. It is an experiment that is worth the effort.

Each section within this book will end with a saying or a Liberian proverb to guide us through our journey to self-awareness.

THOUGHT

An alternative route leads to the same destination.

1

FULL STOCK OF THE "I"

When we point a finger at others, three fingers point back at us. Most of us are so focused on identifying the faults of others that we neglect to evaluate ourselves. When was the last time we took stock of our lives? Effective self-discovery requires us to be honest, trusting, and forgiving -- of others and ourselves. To fully take stock of our lives we must be one hundred percent (100%) honest about everything.

Our journey to self-awareness begins with an inventory of our positive and negative characteristics. Now is the time for each and every one of us to look inward. We will each select a time and place to engage in this exercise in solitude for a set period of time. This process may be done in several sittings so do not rush. Each of us will bring along our favorite "pen or pencil" and three sheets of paper, each bearing a different heading: "The Light," "The Darkness" and "The New Horizon."

We begin with a "scan" of our bodies. We will use our bodies as a guide for our journey through the light and dark areas of our lives. Some parts of the body -- especially the head, the heart and the feet -- provide more information than other areas. For example, the head stores most decisions we have made; our hearts house the feelings of joy and sorrow from those decisions; our feet may take us to beautiful places at one time, or into scary situations at another. These areas of our bodies are a treasure trove for our inventory.

We may start at our heads and work down through our toes, or vice versa. In either case, we will not miss an inch of our body. Do not rush. Imagine that we have x-ray vision, allowing us to see all aspects of our lives. Write down whatever the x-ray images reveal. This can be a word, a phrase or a complete sentence. Write whatever that particular image evokes, and do not erase anything. Sometimes the scan will reveal hurtful things; at other times, it will reveal fond memories. Trust what is revealed and jot it down.

On the page headed "The Light," we will record all our wonderful, nice, lovely and positive traits. On the page headed "The Darkness" we will record our self-absorbed, wicked, and arrogant shortcomings. Finally, we will leave the page headed "The New Horizon" blank. This page will be filled in after the completion of this exercise and time and again throughout our lives. The New Horizon allows us to reach beyond the rainbow and into a brand new light. It will become our personal memoir and a testament to our lives.

After all the necessary data has been gathered, we take a long break to regain our focus. The analysis process requires a fresh mind for accurate evaluation of the data. The review-ing process should take as long as necessary in order for us to come to grips with the information it contains. We must deal with our past in order to truly live in the present.

THOUGHT
Focusing on the bright side of things makes the negative a bit easier to swallow.

2

THE LIGHT

Bright sunshine, aglow, and shimmering are the images that come to mind when thinking of the light. These images evoke warm, tingling sensations throughout our bodies. These are the positive traits we inherited or develop over time.

Listed below are some of the most common positive traits. Take a few minutes to review the list and highlight those that are currently part of our individual arsenals. Feel free to add other positive traits to the list.

Affectionate
Appreciative
Charismatic
Clever
Comforting
Committed

Compassionate
Complimentary
Concerned
Considerate
Creative
Dependable

Empathetic	Loving
Encouragement	Loyal
Flexible	Open
Forgiving	Patient
Generous	Playful
Gentle	Polite
Good listener	Protective
Grateful	Respectful
Helpful	Responsible
Honest	Sense of humor
Humble	Tender
Insightful	Tolerant
Interested	Understanding
Kind	

We will not be daunted by this list. No one person embodies all these virtues. The goal is to develop as many of these virtues as possible. *We are all a work in progress.* All it takes is a little practice and the right attitude.

We recommend the seven traits listed below because they promote compassion and humanity. These traits are essential and are part of the fundamental building blocks of life.

Honesty
Tolerance
Responsibility
Forgiveness
Gratitude
Fairness and Equality
Love and Kindness

An in-depth review of each of these seven traits will broaden our view of how they contribute to our building blocks of life. This solid foundation is what we need to steer us through life. These traits bring a touch of humanity to our lives and set each and every one of us on the right path to a better future.

As we become more in sync with our bodies, we will add other traits that are essential for personal growth; and we will do the same in-depth review as above.

THOUGHT
The light data gives us the illumination we need to deal with darkness. The knowledge and wisdom gained from the light will empower us.

HONESTY

Honesty is uprightness of character and action. It is being straight forward, fair, honorable, and ethical. Honesty is a blessing. We should seek to treat others as we want others to treat us.

Dealing with others in a straightforward manner can take us a long way in life. When we are honest with people, they are (as a general rule) honest with us in return. People like to deal with honest individuals and businesses. We cannot pick and choose when to be honest.

Sometimes we will encounter dishonesty, but that should not give us license to become dishonest in our dealings. Lack of honesty can affect our relationships with our families, our friends, and in our careers. Dishonesty is bound to catch up with us eventually.

As humans, we must work hard to remain honest at all times. Just remember whatever we sow in this life we will surely reap. Remember, dishonesty is not measured by quantity.

Dealing with others in an honest manner moves us ahead in life because an honest deed opens more doors. Honesty is the best policy.

LIBERIAN FOLKLORE
You can run but you can't hide.

"Whatever you do in the dark, will eventually come to light."

TOLERANCE

Tolerance is sympathy for or indulgence in beliefs or practices differing from or conflicting with our own belief. The world we live in needs tolerance more than ever. Tolerance allows others to practice whatever they believe, and feel comfortable doing so. We do not have to agree with someone else's beliefs but we must not impede them. Our way of doing things should not interfere with the way others do things.

We all view life from our own perspective. We may differ in how we analyze what we see, but in the end, our conclusion is the same. All we did was take an alternative approach.

Sometimes we run the risk of becoming intolerant by creating absolute truths, which leave no room for the beliefs and practices of others. Keep in mind: *there are no absolute truths when dealing with human emotions.*

Most of the intolerance we face in society comes from fear of the unknown. We should not be guided by fear; tolerance breeds understanding.

Therefore, take caution when people try to encourage intolerance of others based on their race, religion, economic status, sexual orientation or ethnicity. Heads of states, professors, the media, our parents, friends and even religious leaders often breed such intolerance. For example, some leaders use these tactics as a way to create division within their society in order to solidify their hold on power. We need to see past these tactics with sound judgment based on facts.

Once we learn more about the unknown, we can watch our intolerance dissipate right before our eyes. We have to learn to base decisions on facts. Everyone has heard of the golden rule that says, "Do unto others as you would have others do unto you." Life is funny: the persons or groups we mistreat today might be the persons or groups that determine our future. Our position in life can change in a blink of an eye.

LIBERIAN PROVERB

Eagle fly high, it got to come down to drink muddy water.

(Be careful whom you step on while going up the ladder because you might meet them coming down the ladder.)

RESPONSIBILITY

Responsibility is a moral, legal and mental accountability. It is a way to account for our obligation to ourselves and to our fellow human beings. Responsibility is something that should come easily to everyone of us, but many of us find it difficult to achieve. Responsibility is a personal requirement. We have to be accountable for what we do to others or allow others to do to us. If we cannot take responsibility for our own actions society is at risk of becoming anarchy.

People sometimes say that they are responsible but they are only referring to being responsible for themselves. Responsibility is more than the "I." It applies to all human beings, animals, and the environment we live in.

First, we must be accountable for our own actions. We must own up to the harm we cause others and ourselves. We cannot make excuses for our behavior. The fact that someone else harmed us in the past does not give us the right to do the same to others. If anything, we as individuals should advocate to eliminate such hurt from society. Sometimes, in our pursuit to achieve our goals, we may unintentionally harm others. Every action has a consequence. Owning up to our responsibility keeps us honest.

Second, we are responsible for the children we bring into this world. No matter how children enter this world, once they are born they become our responsibility. We must teach them to be respectful, honest, responsible, fair, tolerant, loving, caring, reliable, patient, understanding and grateful for themselves and others. Children follow the example set by their parents and their surroundings, so be a good role model. Remember, monkey see monkey do.

Third, we are responsible for our neighbors. We have all heard the saying; "it takes a village to raise a child." That is how children are brought up back home in Liberia and other parts of Africa. Everyone looks out for his or her neighbors and their children and vice versa. Most people do not appreciate this system until they are mature adults. This system works because one person cannot be everywhere at all times.

Immigrants to the United States are frequently taken aback by the fact that some Americans tend not to know their neighbors. Most people rationalize that they are too busy to get to know the people living next door. Building a relationship with those who live near us strengthens ties we might need down the road. When people know each other by name, they are more protective of one another. We recommend that everyone take a few minutes to get to know his or her neighbors. Occasionally have a brief conversation even if it is just about the weather. This little interaction might even lead to meaningful friendship or more.

Finally, we are responsible for how we treat the environment. We are part of this earth, and it is our duty to keep it safe for our children, the animals and ourselves. If we continue to mistreat the earth, we will pay dearly for our lack of actions. The air we breathe will cause us to become sick. The lack of care for the environment will cause fire, mudslides, waters shortages, starvation and much more. We depend on the earth to take care of us, and the earth depends on us to take care of her.

THOUGHT
We need to stop shifting blame and
own up to our behaviors and responsibilities.

FORGIVENESS

Forgiveness is letting go of all the anger, resentment and hurt others have caused in our lives. Forgiveness is necessary for personal growth. Most of us find it difficult to forgive because we believe that if we forgive someone that might empower him or her to harm or hurt us again. But, forgiveness is not forgetfulness.

Forgiveness allows us to move forward in life. When we forgive what others have done to us, we unburden our lives, making room for our full self-expression and contribution to the world. When possible, seek forgiveness because it is the only way to cleanse the soul.

In his book about the Holocaust called *The Sunflower: On the Possibilities and Limits of Forgiveness*[1], Simon Wiesenthal writes about who can accept or issue forgiveness on behalf of the dead. Who are we to say that the dead would have forgiven those who committed heinous crimes against them? According to Wiesenthal, only the living survivors of the holocaust can forgive those who harmed them. However, we as a society cannot forgive on behalf of the dead. We can redress the harm done and maybe offer financial restitution, but we cannot accept forgiveness or offer pardon on behalf of the dead.

Only the living can dispense absolution for the crimes committed against them. Therefore, ask for forgiveness from individuals while they are alive because they are the only ones who can truly forgive us.

Sometimes it is impossible to obtain forgiveness from the living, in which case it is up to God to dispense final absolution. But while on this earth, we can make amends through kindness, charity, and by attempting to ensure that such crimes never happen again.

Not forgiving is a heavy load to bear; hatred takes away from our happiness and limits our lives. If we have the chance to forgive those who have harmed us, we should seize the opportunity. Remember, only victims of a crime can forgive both the living and the dead.

THOUGHT

Forgive but never forget. If we forget,
history is bound to repeat itself.

No matter how bad our past may have been, we need to con-front it and make peace with it. It might require us to forgive others and ourselves because that's the only way we can truly move forward and live in the present. Forgiveness releases us from the chain that binds us thus allowing us to soar.

GRATITUDE

Gratitude is the feeling of thankfulness and appreciation. Sometimes we take life for granted. Just the fact that we are alive should inspire us to feel grateful. However, being grateful is often difficult. We are all guilty of ingratitude. We spend most of our time focusing on what others have, and we forget to cherish what we have in our own lives.

While some people living in third world countries are grateful for a cup of clean drinking water, we complain about such trivialities such as tardy buses, late trains, or cancelled flights. To some, missing the bus, the train, or the plane could mean the difference between life and death. The fact that the buses, trains, or planes will eventually come is cause to be grateful. Some people living in other parts of the world do not have such concerns because there are no buses, trains or airplanes.

No matter how bad our current situation is, we should be grateful. We are not all going to be rich. So do not let the ads, infomercials and the how-to-become-a-millionaire books tell us otherwise. That does not mean that we are not talented or intelligent. Some people are luckier in life than others or have the right connections in life. Others work hard to earn everything they have by taking every opportunity that comes their way. They do not constantly brood over what they do not have in their lives. They take action by walking their talk.

Most of us sit around holding pity parties for ourselves until we are pinned into a corner before taking action. The only time we become truly grateful is when we are either sick or in a near-death situation. These are the times we recall the good things we have in our lives. During these situations, we submit to the God we serve to spare our lives. We promise to be more grateful for everything. However, as humans, our memories are very short, and we soon go back to our ungrateful ways.

Riches cannot be measured by money and owned objects alone. We are richer when we have people to share our lives with, and people who truly love us no matter our faults. The challenges we encounter in life make us stronger. They help us discover new solutions to problems and allow us to reinvent ourselves and evolve.

Gratitude is especially important during these tough economic times. During these hard times, all of our worldly possessions could easily slip through our hands. We need to accept our current situations but set goals to improve upon them. Envying others for what they have is a dangerous game. Remember we are blessed in our own unique ways.

SONG
"Count your blessings name them one by one."

We cannot count all of our blessings because they are too many.

LOVE and KINDNESS

Love and kindness are two strong positive emotions of regard and affection -- the act of being warmhearted, considerate, and sympathetic. *The Bible asks us to love our neighbors as we love ourselves.* It is that simple. While this is simple enough guidance, it is not so easy to follow, especially when -- as is often the case in the Industrialized Countries -- people do not know their neighbors. How can we love others if we do not take five minutes to get to know them?

In general, we are a loving and kind people, but our love and kindness applies mostly to our families and a limited group of people. We should move beyond our inner circle of friends and explore the world outside of our comfort zone.

When we withhold love and kindness based on class, race, sexual orientation, economic status, religion or ethnicity, we are being greedy with our heart. We should love everyone no matter his or her station in life.

We tend to exclude people based on their race, religion, sexual orientation, economic status or ethnicity. What kind of love and kindness is that? Our love and kindness should sometimes make us feel uncomfortable. For example, we should invite into our homes, churches or social gatherings those whom society looks down upon. If we are unable to bring them into our homes, then we should take time to visit them at homeless shelters, hospitals or orphanages.

In addition, always speak to everyone in a dignified manner. Treat everyone with love, kindness, and respect. Never talk down to anyone. A person can be poor in worldly possessions, but rich in dignity. When we withhold our love and kindness from others, we are taking away the one thing they do possess. Once a person's dignity is stripped away, that person ceases to exist. We do not know what circumstances brought them to this point in their life, so we need to be tolerant, because we too could end up in the same situation. If we treat everyone with love and kindness, this world will be a much better place.

THOUGHT

We should open ourselves up to everyone because we never know who will be there when we are truly in need.

FAIRNESS and EQUALITY

Fairness and equality are states of being essentially equal or equivalent: social state of affairs in which all people within a specific society or isolated group have the same status in a certain respect. Fairness and equality are not part of some a la carte menu. We should measure it by how we would like others to treat or judge us. Therefore, we should practice fairness and equality at all times.

How do we determine what is just or unjust? In most cases, individuals in positions of power or control determine fairness and equality. If they lack moral integrity, then their views on fairness and equality are skewed, and unjust treatment might result. In those situations, we must stand for fairness and equality no matter the consequences. Sometimes to achieve fairness and equality individuals must die, be imprisoned and/or harmed.

If heroes such as Martin Luther King Jr., Abraham Lincoln, Mahatma (Mohandas Karamchand) Gandhi, Rosa Parks, Nelson Mandela, and the Dalai Lama did not risk their lives for their causes, where would we be now? They did it to improve the lives of their families and their respective peoples. They knew the punishment that awaited them, but their commitment to fairness and equality far outweighed their need for personal safety and comfort.

As we move through time, we must remember the suffering and sacrifices of such individuals. We should celebrate them and cherish them and the fruits of their labor. We can never forget and we can never give up on fairness and equality for all. Remember: one mistreated individual or group is one too many.

The blood, tears, and sacrifice of those who came before us should not be in vain. We should instead expand and build upon these causes for the next generation. It is our job to make sure everyone is treated fairly.

THOUGHT

Life is funny because one minute we're on top and the next minute we've hit rock bottom.

Be kind to everyone. Those we least expect might very well become our knight in shining armor.

Now we are certain that these seven traits above are essential for our personal growth. They enhance our good qualities and bring us a step closer to the light and the horizon.

3

THE DARKNESS

Gloomy, dreadful, dim, and murky are images that come to mind when thinking about the darkness. Evoking scary, horrible vibrations throughout our bodies, these dark images cause many to hide themselves behind walls. These images prevent full expression and interaction with the rest of society.

Darkness represents the negative attributes that we acquire along our paths in life. Negative characteristics are learned behaviors; and that is the good news, because learned behaviors *can be unlearned*. So do not say '*that's just who I am*' because those bad behaviors can be unlearned.

Below are some common negative characteristics. Take a minute to review the list and highlight those that apply.

Apathetic	Inefficiency
Brutal	Injustice
Closed-minded	Intimidating
Cold-hearted	Intolerance
Critical	Judgmental
Cruel	Lazy
Dishonest	Mean-spirited
Disingenuous	Pessimistic
Disloyal	Rude
Egotistic	Thankless
Faultfinding	Thoughtless
Heartless	Troublesome
Hurtful	Unpredictability
Impatient	Violence
Indifferent	Vindictive

The dark side is a place we have all traveled at some point in our lives. Our negative behaviors come to light during tough times or situations. During these dark periods, we should try instead to focus on the positive. This requires a lot of effort and persistence on our part. Our negative vices erode our building blocks and set us back in life. Below are five traits that are extremely harmful because they destroy our solid foundation and place us on shaky ground. We recommend eliminating these five traits from our lives.

Vindictiveness
Rudeness
Pessimism
Judgmental
Close-mindedness

We will review these five traits and show how devastating they are in our lives. These negative traits set us back in our pursuit of inner peace and stop us from reaching the new horizons.

Feel free to add other negative traits that impede upon our solid foundation. But do the same in-depth review as described above to truly understand the cause and effect of these negative traits.

THOUGHT

Darkness clouds our visions with negativity that causes us to make irrational decisions. We should move into the sunlight so we can make rational decisions and see clearly.

VINDICTIVENESS

Vindictiveness is a malevolent desire for revenge. Cruelty is something we have all experienced at one time or another. Our first reaction is to seek revenge against those who have harmed or mistreated us. As children, we are taught to defend ourselves. Our upbringings cause us to react first and think later. We cannot permit this to become our philosophy for life as it is ultimately self-defeating.

Instead, our first reaction might be to try to understand why people act in such a manner. For example, sometimes what we thought was harm done to us was done unintentionally. What we perceived as hurtful might be accidental.

Instead of plotting revenge, we should let the offenders know how their behaviors affect us. Understanding whether something was done intentionally is more important because it will allow us to react appropriately. We should learn to step back a little from a tense situation to understand the facts before taking any action. We must learn to restrain ourselves in heated situations.

If a situation truly gets out of hand, the best policy is to either walk away or seek help. We should not let others make us do things that we might regret for the rest of our lives. We should stand up for ourselves but with an appropriate response. We are responsible for our own action.

THOUGHTS
Getting even is only a temporary solution. We should look for the underlying causes of offensive behaviors in order to obtain permanent solutions.

RUDENESS

Rudeness is a behavior that is intentionally discourteous, indifferent, insulting, and lacking in social refinement. Rudeness is something that is extremely unattractive. People can be beautiful or handsome, but rudeness transforms their beauty into ugliness. There is no need to be rude. What do we achieve from being ignorant, indifferent, or intentionally discourteous? We achieve nothing except heartaches and headaches from such behaviors.

As a matter of fact, ignorant people often lack confidence and hide behind their rudeness. If we are sure of ourselves, we are more considerate and understanding of the feelings and needs of others. It takes a lot to be impolite and rude.

The main question is how does such a behavior affect others? When we are rude to others, we take away a piece of their dignity by our behaviors. We belittle them in the presence of other people who might look up to them. Our behavior might affect them for years to come. Rudeness gets us nowhere in life. The next time we think about being hurtful and rude to others, we should instead try to be a little gracious and understanding.

WISDOM

Never make a person feel less than a human being even when they have hit rock bottom. Their dignity is all they have and it should remain intact.

Courtesy of my dear father Varney

PESSIMISM

Pessimism is the certainty that things will turn out badly, and the tendency to stress the negative. Pessimism is a state of mind. We all have traveled down this road in our lives. This is where we go when we are battling with life's challenges. Whenever things around us get hard, we begin to view the world from a dejected point of view. Are we really at a disadvantage?

We might experience our current situation as "out of control" but it is better to see the glass half-full than half-empty. If the glass is half-empty, then there is less hope and we fall further into despair. The fact that we are alive gives us another opportunity to start anew because everyday offers up a clean slate.

According to Zora Neale Hurston, *Their Eyes Were Watching God*[2], possibilities exist just beyond the horizon. All it takes is persistence and courage to know that things are bound to get better. It might take years, but we have to believe in ourselves through it all. We should not allow pride to stand in our way. We must have hope that we will overcome and rise above the tide.

The fact is that in life, everyone will experience bumps along the way but that is just a part of life. No matter how much money, friends, or family we have, heartaches and headaches will find us. That is *Life 101*. However, how we overcome these adversities in our lives will tell us what we are truly made off.

Those who are pessimists will always have difficulties, if not impossible times, trying to overcome adversities because they have a doomsday approach to life. Their view of life is so negative that they cannot see anything else. If our outlook on life is dim, how can we see what is on the horizon?

In order for us to see what lies ahead, we must strive to be more optimistic about life. Optimism allows us to experience the world from a positive perspective and to look for the good in others. This helps us overcome adversities that come into our lives and helps us move beyond our own difficulties. We will experience many speed bumps in the future but our new optimism will help make those speed bumps a little bit smoother. We know that after the darkness, comes the light.

COMMON SAYING

If at first you don't succeed, try, try, and try again.

Never give up on yourself.

JUDGMENTAL

To be Judgmental is to exhibit a tendency to critique harshly. Judging others comes so easily to many of us, an automatic part of our subconscious of which we may not even be aware. We tell ourselves it is not good to judge a book by its cover, but we do it all the time. How does judging others affect our lives? When we are being judgmental, we risk letting good people slip through our lives simply because we made a snap decision about them.

We mostly judge others based on their appearance. For example, if someone is wearing a hooded sweatshirt then that person must be a thug but upon closer examination, the person believed to be a thug might be the executive of a major company. On the other hand, the person wearing the three-piece suit might turn out to be the thug. We need to look beyond superficial appearances and learn the substance of the individual. We can start by greeting everyone we encounter.

Sometimes we need to turn beyond the first page of a book before coming to an initial conclusion. It might be a page-turner or the next best seller. This simple act will allow us to base our decision to associate or not on substance rather than mere appearances. In practical terms we could meet our husband, wife or new best friend. Best advise, withhold initial judgment and learn a little about that individual before coming to a final conclusion.

<u>THOUGHT</u>

Appearances can be deceiving because there are many people playing dress-up to trap those impressed with appearances.

Not everything that sparkles is made of gold, diamond, or platinum because some are made of fool's gold.

CLOSE-MINDEDNESS

Close-mindedness is intolerance of the beliefs and opinions of others and a stubborn lack of receptivity to new ideas. Close-mindedness impedes not only our lives but also the lives of those with whom we associate. When we are closed-minded, we stop learning new things. Having our own ideology is a good thing, but we should be willing to expand our minds and our views of society.

Insisting on our own ideology at any cost prevents us from moving ahead in our jobs, schools and in all other aspects of our lives. We are limited to our tainted views of the world. We do not change as society progresses because that would require us to learn something new. We do not need to abandon our core values in order to learn, grow, and evolve.

What we believed in when we were teenagers may no longer be appropriate as we move into adulthood. Our life experiences often change our view of the world. As long as we are heading in a positive direction, we should allow ourselves to progress.

Once we have eliminated close-mindedness, our vision of the world will be clear, and we will see the world for what it is and not what we would like it to be. This will allow us to move forward and be more receptive to new things, new people and new ideas.

THOUGHT

Open your mind to the unexpected and explore the wonders of life – it might surprise you by its beauty.

"When I was a child, I spoke like a child, thought like a child, reasoned like a child; when I became a man, I did away with childish things."

I Corinthians 13:11

The above review highlights how destructive these five traits are in our lives. They set us back and move us further away from the horizon and deeper into the darkness. We must do everything within our power to eliminate these traits in order to reach just beyond the horizon.

4

THE BUSINESS PLAN

As humans, we need goals and the strategies for implementing these goals. A business plan is a roadmap used by businesses to move towards desired outcomes. Our aim is to create a viable business plan for our lives. The same principles that guide a business apply to life. We will use our current situations as our points of reference.

Based on our current situations we will create a strategy for obtaining and maintaining our goals for the future. As in life, a good business plan tests for feasibility. Once feasibility is established, the plan becomes our workable roadmap. The roadmap can then be altered along the way to accommodate changes in our lives.

A good business reevaluates its plan from time to time to eliminate those aspects that are not working and improve upon those that are working. Just like a business, we should reevaluate our lives every so often. We must eliminate people or things that impede our growth and keep those that encourage us in every aspect of our lives. For this exercise, we will use a simple business plan format. A business plan consists of:

- Executive Summary
- Ownership
- Description of Business
- Market Information
- Financial Information

EXECUTIVE SUMMARY

The executive summary is a brief two-page overview of our lives. It includes our goals and strategies and a plan for achieving them. This section summarizes the details of the entire plan precisely. The executive summary consists of the mission statement, goals and objectives, and keys to success.

First, write a mission statement of no more than thirty words. This is our personal introduction or commercial that conveys a glimpse of our personality, our purpose on earth and the principles that will guide our path.

Second, the goals and objectives describe how our mission will be implemented. These include markers and milestones to be set in advance. This process allows us to highlight achievements and goals reached. Typical markers and milestones are yearly, monthly and weekly.

Finally, keys to success define the short and long-term results or outcomes by which we measure our progress towards our goals. Short-term outcomes are those we expect to accomplish within a given period of time as we move towards our long-range vision.

Long-term outcomes are those that range from as little as a year to several years or even decades. We will establish our life philosophy and create firm markers and milestones to celebrate achievements.

After reading the executive summary, it should demonstrate the workability of our plan, and why our life makes sense, and the direction in which we are headed. The executive summary conveys an accurate overview of all our wishes, dreams and goals for the future. While some of these might change as we progress through life, this initial summary provides a frame of reference to guide us through, and to pull us back if and when we fall off track.

If the objective of the executive summary is achieved then our hat is off to each and every one of us, well done!

THOUGHT

A plan is a point of reference -- it is not etched in stone.

OWNERSHIP

Several types of legal entities exist as a structure to advance our mission in life. These include Sole Proprietorship, Partnership, and Limited Liability Corporations (LLC). These legal entities have different risk components and advantages, similar to life. Which one of these entities fits what we envision for our life? Most companies pick the business entity that best fits their vision. They have calculated all the advantages and disadvantages of that entity.

Sole Proprietorship (SP) is a form of business that encompasses a lot of personal risk but allows a startup company to exist under its owner's name. Sole proprietorship means retaining ownership one hundred percent of the time.

In such a business, we direct all the comings and goings of our lives. All the rewards and the risks are shouldered personally. Depending on the level of risk, we could lose it all, but we could also receive many accolades for our hard work. This type of entity is not for the weak-willed but for the more adventuresome.

For people who live for the excitement and thrill of taking risk this form of entity may best fit their lifestyle. These people are willing to bet it all on one throw at a roulette table. Their motto "easy come, easy go."

Is a Sole Proprietor the best we can be? Can we protect ourselves and still have control of our destiny? Only we can decide.

Partnership allows more than one person to form a business using an operating agreement. Married couples are an obvious example of partnership. A good partnership has an operating agreement from the start that assigns roles for each person and their contribution to the company. Setting initial rules and regulations or expectations eliminates misunderstandings down the road. The vows taken between married couples serve as their operating agreement.

There are two types of partnership, **General Partnership (GP)** and **Limited Liability Partnership (LLP).** Limited Liability Partnership provides legal protection of personal assets while General Partnership does not.

The GP and LLP partnership entities are good options for those individuals who cannot function as a one-man show. But seriously, a company sometimes requires intellectual property from some members and financing from others. This pooling of resources is something necessary to sustain us.

A Limited Liability Partnership creates a perfect avenue for a partnership. This form of entity is good for the conservatives among us because it allows them to spread the risk. Conservatives take minimum risk if possible. This form of partnership offers the legal protection of assets

On the other hand, a General Partnership is like a Sole Proprietorship, with no protection of personal assets. General Partnership is like marriage without the prenuptial agreement. There's nothing wrong with this but it leaves everyone with exposure to liability.

The disadvantage with a partnership model is if one person does something bad or disagreements arise, the entire business might be in jeopardy. That is why detailed partnership and operating agreements must be in place. The General Partnership motto is the same as Sole Proprietorship, while the Limited Liability Partnership motto is "Any protection is better than none." Who are we, General Partnerships (GP) or Limited Liability Partnerships (LLP)?

Last but not least is the Limited Liability Corporation (LLC) that protects our personal assets, and allows us to take risks. Both an individual and/or a group can operate as a Limited Liability Corporation.

As singles, the LLC allows us to take risks with some form of protection. This business model is like venture capital, which provides financing that allows for more innovation for experimental business or business concepts. As long as we are honest in our dealings we can sleep at night and know we are protected, and we can push the envelope when it comes to development and groundbreaking ideas.

Singles or couples who are not married should keep their finances separate. If possible, money should not commingle except to pay bills jointly. We should be open to all the wonders another person can bring into our lives but we should be wise in how to protect ourselves. Learn the substance of another individual but neither jump the gun nor make snap decisions.

Limited Liability Corporations are for all the adventurous, the conservatives, the liberals and the weak-hearted. Their motto is "better safe than sorry." Limited Liability Corporations relish the fact that they have the freedom to adjust the level of risk taken at any given moment.

What form of legal entity will we pick and why? Are we a SP, GP, LLP or LLC? We should base our decision on the amount of risk we are willing to take in our lives. How will we assign responsibility between, for example, a husband and a wife? Will we establish the same standard used by businesses between owners and employees?

Remember, owners are those who can independently control their destiny, while employees depend on their owners. We must answer these questions before moving forward in life.

We should set up rules in our lives but they should not be too rigid. Rigid rules do not allow us to grow and do not allow for mistakes. In life, we will make mistakes; more important we still learn from them. Let us go beyond the black and white and into the gray. We need to think and do things outside the box.

Remember, intentional fraud is not protected. Life is what we make of it. Nothing in life is guaranteed.

THOUGHT

A General Partnership is like a marriage without a prenuptial agreement and a Limited Liability Partnership is like one with a prenuptial agreement.

DESCRIPTION OF BUSINESS

The description of the business is a historical overview of the products, management and those involved in the running of the business. This should include the inner workings of the "company." This description should include:

- History of the business   (History of life)

- Role in the business   (Role we play in life)

- Product and Service   (What we offer the world)

HISTORY OF THE BUSINESS

The history of a business should be an overview from its inception to the present. It should be a brief history about our parents before and after we were born. We should know who they are and how they met.

The door to the world sprung open on the day we were each born. Now that we are here, tell the world about our time on this earth and things we have encountered along the way.

What struggles have we encountered? How did our parents make us wiser or stronger in our pursuit of our dreams and desires? During the low periods, did we think we might never rise above the tide? Once we made it, were we proud of our inner strength and endurance? If anything, the hard times should have taught us how to overcome and believe in the new horizon.

Be sure to highlight the achievements and good times we have had in life. Were our parents and loved ones proud of our achievements? Who were the people who encouraged and supported us every step of the way? Did they love us in spite of our faults?

Like the food squirrels stow away for the hard winter months ahead, recording the good times helps sustain us when hard times and headaches come knocking on our doors. Treasure these memories. Occasionally, peek at these memories and the events surrounding them and have a good-hearted laugh.

Now bring us up-to-date on current events. What progress have we each made towards achieving our dreams? Are we where we thought we would be? Or, did life throw us a curve that altered our dreams along the way? Are we happy with our current situation? If not, do we plan to change it?

Happiness is essential to any plan because we could realize our dreams and still be unhappy. Sometimes what we plan turns out differently in real life. Just as in life, a happy business environment leads to better returns. Happiness is the key to a successful life.

THOUGHT

When deciding on a career, we should pick something that makes us happy, instead of what will make us rich. It is good to be happy and rich, instead of rich and miserable.

ROLE IN THE BUSINESS

Every business has a different hierarchy and some members play multiple roles. The roles members provide to the company depend on their level of activity, contribution, and knowledge. Life is the same way. We can either be an active member of life or a passive observer. What role will we play in our lives?

Some of us are active members in our daily lives. We make sure we are present and accounted for. We do what is asked of us, and we follow up with those accountable to us. We help in our communities and stay abreast of what is happening locally and internationally. We are the Chief Executive Officers (CEOs) of our lives, and we take our role seriously.

Others are passive observers of their lives. Their motto is "I don't care." Their attitude is a reflection of their motto.

Just as the director directs the actors in movie or the conductor conducts an orchestra, these people wait for others to direct their lives. They glide through life without care, yet they are dependent on everyone around them.

This mere fact leaves them at the mercy of others and into the hands of those who seek to control them. When we depend too much on others, we give them the power to manipulate us. Asking others for help is fine as long as we are not depending on them for everything. We must trust our abilities to conduct our own lives.

The roles we play in life determine our success. Success is not always measured by financial rewards but the pure joy of achieving a goal. We are the only ones who can truly advocate our issues because we understand what makes us tick.

We get out of life what we put into it. The best way for us to achieve our dreams is to become the owner and CEO of our destiny. Remember a good business depends on all its members playing an active role.

THOUGHT

If we do not know who we are, where we come from, others will mold us into what they want and expect of us.

Believe in ourselves.

PRODUCTS and SERVICES

Products are the tangible things a business has to offer its customers; services are the Intellectual Property (IP) that a company provides to its clients. A good product-based company offers a product that meets its customers' needs by using creative packaging and unique concepts. A service-based company provides the latest and best IP to its clients. That means keeping abreast of the latest technology and advancements in its field to ensure clients are receiving the latest information. These two concepts, product-based and service-based models also apply to life.

Products are the tangible things we have to offer the world. This can be as simple as a smile. This simple gesture can make a difference in a person's life. We can contribute financially, through our donations to charity, family or friends.

Taking responsibility is another way to increase the value of our "brand" and our visibility in the world. What does that look like? We must show up to work, meetings, appointments and other events on time. Be dependable. When we market ourselves like any good brand, and are dependable in our delivery, others will invest in our lives.

Service is the knowledge we have obtained either through formal education and/or from life. Some call this "wisdom." Some people are not educated but they are very knowledgeable and wise. Education is important but it is not all we need to navigate through life.

In life, we have all come across those individuals who are extremely well educated but lacking in common sense. All they have is book knowledge. They can help us explain the law, dissect a book, or talk about philosophy all day long.

These individuals will need someone with common sense to help them weave their paths through life.

Sometimes experience trumps formal education. Those without any formal education can be extremely knowledgeable about how life works. They may not have a degree, but they have what we call "street smarts." They have lived and experienced life, first hand. Their knowledge comes from experiences and from the depth of their souls. But they too will at times need someone with education, something they lack, to guide them.

Everybody has a purpose in life. Education should not be a requirement for association. Exclusion of any kind is risky business because we might miss something exciting and enlightening. At some level we all offer products and services.

Some of us have more products than services or vice versa. We should exploit our advantages and improve upon our weaknesses and use our abilities to the utmost each and every day.

THOUGHT

Inclusion opens our horizons to the world beyond our imagination.

MARKETING INFORMATION

Successful companies know that branding is the key to success. Marketing communicates to the world that we have arrived. How we market ourselves determines how far we get in life.

The image we project is how others see us and determines who we are. Almost every athlete, actor, or model has an image consultant to help them project a certain image in order to become successful.

We should treat ourselves as a business entity in a professional setting. In business, we should carry ourselves in a professional manner and be respectful and courteous to all.

Marketing allows others to see us at our best. We cannot project one image and expect others to treat us contrary to that image. Misrepresentation of ourselves is a mistake.

We should not be afraid to let our light shine. Project the image that we would like others to see and one that pleases us as well.

THOUGHT
There is no brand better than oneself.

FINANCIAL INFORMATION

We may not want to focus on money but like it or not, money does make the world go around. We need money to survive in this world. Financial literacy is something parents should teach their children from an early age.

Those with trust funds might not believe they have need of financial literacy but we beg to differ. If they do not know how to manage money, it is only a matter of time before they blow their entire trust funds right down to zero. Individuals with trust funds have an upper hand because they do not have to work to acquire money. However, they still need to know how to manage it.

For the rest of the population, those without trust funds, the question is, how do we support ourselves? This is a serious question and we have to be realistic about it. We cannot depend on our good friends at *"Visa," "MasterCard," "Discover,"* and *"American Express"* because they require that we repay with interest. Credit cards should only be used in true emergencies.

Are we going to be financially independent or dependent on others?

Some of us work hard to earn our keep. We are willing to do any job in order to meet our needs. No matter what job is, we should take pride in whatever we do for a living. We should not compare our job to that of others.

Our current job may not be our ideal job but we may need it to survive. In this case, we should have a plan to find something else that aligns us with our ideal job. As long as we are at this current job, we should give it our all. We should earn a living by doing an honest day's work.

Then there are the parents who would rather stay at home and care for their children. They are willing to give up their professions for the sake of the children. In some cases, it makes financial sense to have one parent raise the kids while the other works outside the home. Whatever the situation, these people are trading one job for another. Taking care of children is more than a full-time. These parents are independent because they are doing more than a professional day's work.

Finally, we have the dependent people who sit around and expect others to take care of them. They are trading in their freedom for money. In most of these situations, the person with the money is calling all the shots. However, people in these situations do not mind that fact as long as they can shop, party, travel and generally enjoy the wealth supplied by another.

There's nothing free in this world; they are trading their freedom of choice for a lifestyle. There is nothing wrong with this lifestyle as long as everyone agrees to the terms. Nevertheless, the risks are high. Any sense of "freedom" in this scenario is false: such dependent people are frequently told how to behave in most situations, and are easily traded for someone new. When traded, they are left with no plan for the future and no resources to fall back on.

We should all strive to be independent or semi-independent because we never know what can happen in life. We should plan for the unexpected. No matter how much money our parents or our partners make, we should be self-sufficient. We should know what is happening regarding our finances and not leave it up to others. Remember, we are the CEOs of our lives.

THOUGHT

Learning the real value of money will aid us in our decisions to become independent or dependent people.

5

PEACE WITHIN

The main point of self-discovery is to find peace within ourselves. While we may not have conquered all of our many demons, we have become aware of them. We have learned tools to figure them out and put in place steps to control or deal with them. This process should have cleansed us of most of our negativity.

We are now at a comfortable place in our lives because we are content with who we are and our current situation. We are comfortable in our skin, and we have set higher goals for our future. Our future goals are about us, and not a competition to obtain what others have in their lives.

We will not envy others for what they have. We do not know how they obtained their wealth. We are all blessed in our unique ways, and we have accepted that as a fact.

We control our own destinies because we are aware of what is happening around us. Like a business, we have picked the entities that fit our personality and lifestyle. We are either pure risk-takers or we are risk-takers who nonetheless like having some security.

Money issues are under control. We keep our eyes on our money and manage our own affairs. We know basic personal finance, and we realize that our financial practices affect every aspect of our lives. We set budgets to obtain our goals.

We move from the darkness and into the light. Our view of the world is from an optimistic lens. We live in the real world and know how to deal with real world situations. We have no illusions as to what might await us down the road but we are confident that our positive outlook and our self-awareness will see us through.

We found peace within because we are comfortable with who we are and where we are heading. We love ourselves "AS IS." We are happy in life. We look beyond the horizon and we see the rainbow. We have arrived. We can now plan our future beyond "The New Horizon" and we will continue to walk our talk.

THOUGHT

We love the person staring back at us in the mirror. We are ready to begin anew with a positive outlook on life.

6

THE NEW HORIZON

We will each write our own memoir about the positive life we plan to live. We will be realistic about all the trials and tribulations we might encounter. Nevertheless, we will let the world know that these difficulties will not sway us from being optimistic. We will walk our talk and set our goals beyond the horizon and reach for the unlimited possibility.

7

AFTERTHOUGHT

Now, let us look at two of the strongest "hot-button" issues that tend to bring out the worst in people -- race and religion.

Race: the topic of race is so sensitive that people are afraid to express their feelings on this matter. Why are we so afraid of the skin color of others? If we really look, our color is the only thing that differentiates us. Do we really believe the skin color of others can harm us? No, it is not the skin color of others that scares us but the attributions we associate with that particular skin color.

Racism is a form of socialization. No one is born a racist. It is a form of indoctrination that people learn at an early age. Most people hate a particular race because their grand-parents, parents or friends expressed disdain for that race. Racism has become a sick form of inheritance that is passed down from one generation to another. We should allow people to express their feelings in an informed way on the subject of race, and we can, in turn, seek to educate them.

Religion: Contrary to its intent to unite and guide us, and promote good will, religion often ends up being a lightning rod waiting to strike at any moment.

People tend to believe that their God is the only true God. It's okay to believe that we are worshipping the one an only true God, but that is our personal opinion and belief. Believing in God -- or not -- is a personal matter. If we focus our spiritual energy on living with integrity, maybe we can stop worrying about which God is the true God. God can fight His own battles; He is a miracle worker in every religion. All we can do is, educate others about our religion and the rest is up to them to decide.

<u>SAYING</u>
United we stand, untied we fall.

1   Simon Wiesenthal, The Sunflower: On the Possibilities and Limits of Forgiveness, 1976 (Schocken)
2   Zora Neale Hurston, The Eyes Were Watching God, 1937 (J.B. Lippincott, Inc.)